She Sows

A Bog Series Novel

By

B. K. Anderson

Copyright Page

ISBN:9798993853161

Printed in the United States of America

Dedication

For those who understand

that life does not dominate life—

it listens, responds,

and grows together.

Epigraph

Life does not begin with control.

It begins with willingness.

The Bog Series

She Stirs

She Seeks

She Sows

Author's Note

She Sows continues the quiet journey begun in *She Stirs* and *She Seeks*.

This story explores what happens after understanding—when knowledge becomes responsibility, and connection becomes action.

The world does not ask to be saved.

It asks to be honored.

Table of Contents

Prologue

What Remains Awake

The bog did not change quickly.

That was how Saxifraga knew the listening had taken hold.

Cycles passed—slow, deliberate, uncounted—and the basin before them remained much as it had been when Asa first crossed into it. Growth continued without surge. Moisture moved through familiar channels. Light fell, withdrew, and returned without insistence. Nothing hurried to prove itself restored.

But the thinning did not return.

Saxifraga felt the difference most clearly in what no longer required her attention. The constant, low vigilance she carried since awakening eased, not into absence, but into trust. The world no longer hovered at the edge of withdrawal. It held itself.

That mattered.

Asa sensed it as well, though he would not have named it that way. He moved through the living basin with the same care he had carried on Earth, stepping where the ground accepted him, pausing when it did not. The alignment within him did not pull forward anymore. It settled, like a note released from tension and allowed to find its natural place in a larger chord.

"This isn't finished," he said once, not as concern but as observation.

"No," Saxifraga agreed. "It has only become possible."

They worked without instruction.

They did not attempt repair. They did not introduce corrections. Where the bog gathered, they waited. Where they hesitated, they listened. The living systems responded to Asa readily—not because he acted, but because he did not insist. Where he remained present, coherence deepened. Where he withdrew, it held.

The world was remembering itself.

Yet remembrance alone was not continuity.

Saxifraga felt the limits of the change even as she honored it. The bog's resonance had stabilized, but it remained narrow. Life here could persist again—but only within a careful range. Growth beyond that would require something more than presence.

It would require renewal.

One-of-One registered the condition without commentary.

Listening sustained, it reported.

Expansion parameters remain unmet.

"Yes," Saxifraga replied. "As expected,"

The message that had stirred at the end of the seeking did not yet resolve. It remained folded within the greater field—faint, patient, and unmistakably intentional. Not a summons. Not a warning.

A signal waiting to be answered.

Asa felt it too, though distantly, like pressure behind a change in weather. He did not ask about it. He had learned that some questions closed doors simply by being formed too soon.

They stood together at the basin's edge, watching light move across the living surface.

"This world can listen now," Asa said. "But it can't teach itself what comes next."

Saxifraga inclined her head slightly. "No. That must be carried in."

"From Earth," he said.

"From many places," she replied. "Earth remembers how to begin. Others will remember how to continue."

The realization settled between them, unforced.

The bog did not require a savior.

It required seed.

Not domination.

Not design.

Participation.

Far beyond the basin, across distances that no longer behaved as separation, One-of-One registered a new alignment. The dormant network did not awaken fully—but several listening points shifted, adjusting orientation as though recognizing a familiar cadence returning to the field.

Markers long placed into time were stirring.

Not opening.

Preparing.

The era of seeking had ended.

What followed would not arrive as discovery.

It would have to be sown.

Chapter One

The Ride

The fold did not want to leave.

Asa had expected motion—some sign that the world had been set aside. A lurch, a lift, a pressure in the bones the way storms changed the air. Instead, the moment of departure arrived as a quiet rearrangement, as if the space around him had decided to behave differently without announcing its choice.

He stood within the stone circle beside Saxifraga. The markings beneath the moss held steady. The trees at the clearing's edge did not lean away. Even the wind continued its small errands through leaf and branch.

Then the sense of *here* loosened.

Not fading. Not breaking. Simply releasing its claim that it was the only place that mattered.

Asa drew in a breath and felt the alignment within him settle into a shape he could not name. It did not pull him forward. It did not tug him back. It held him balanced, the way his body sometimes balanced itself before his mind understood what it was adjusting to.

Saxifraga did not touch him. She did not direct him. She stood just outside the ring as she had before, her posture open, her attention precise.

"You may step out," she said softly, "and the gate will close."

Asa nodded. "I know."

He did not step out.

He stepped deeper in.

The stones did not brighten. The air did not shimmer. The world did not give him the courtesy of spectacle. But the space within the circle tightened, not in confinement, but in focus—like a lens turning toward clarity.

For a moment Asa felt both worlds at once.

Earth did not vanish behind him; it remained present in a way that made him think of the hives when the lid was lifted—still there, still humming, even when he had stepped back and closed it again. The living did not stop because he moved away from it. It carried on, steadier than any fear could argue.

Then the fold gathered.

It was not opening in front of him. It was an inward shift, drawing distance into correspondence. The ground beneath his boots softened in attention without losing its firmness. The carved lines under the moss did not change their shape, only their meaning.

Asa's stomach did not drop. His ears did not pop. His skin did not prickle.

He simply found that the next breath belonged to another gravity.

He opened his eyes and the sky above him was not Earth's.

The light was similar—pale, angled, filtered by atmosphere—
but thinner, as if it had traveled farther to reach him and had
arrived careful not to force itself through. The air carried
moisture without heat. The scent was not floral, not earthy in
the way he knew. It was alive, but it did not advertise its life. It
held it.

Saxifraga stood beside him now.

The gate behind them was not gone, but it had returned to
stillness, its work completed without ceremony. Stone met
moss. Moss met air. Nothing declared what had happened.

Ahead, the bog lay like a held breath.

Asa had imagined a swamp. He had pictured water, mud, and
rot. What he saw instead was a basin of living surfaces layered
like skin—growth upon growth, each strand responsive to the

next, as though the entire place were a single organism that had learned to spread itself thin and wide without losing coherence.

The ground did not feel dead beneath him. It felt like *listening*.

He took a careful step, more out of respect than caution. The surface yielded by a fraction—not sinking, not collapsing, but acknowledging weight the way a living thing acknowledged a touch.

He stopped.

The bog did not react the way animals reacted. It did not startle. It did not flee. It did not move toward him with hunger.

It adjusted.

That adjustment passed through the basin as if the world itself had changed posture, shifting its attention from general to particular. The life nearest Asa altered its orientation, not edging away, not reaching forward—simply turning the way plants turned toward light.

Asa felt the alignment within him widen.

The steadiness he had carried since Saxifraga's arrival did not tighten into urgency. It settled deeper, threading outward into the field around him as naturally as his breath threaded into his body. He had the strange impression that nothing was being taken from him, and nothing was being demanded.

He was being *included*.

Saxifraga watched in stillness.

"The bog recognizes you," she said quietly.

Asa looked at her. "It feels like it's… making room."

"Yes," she replied. "Not because you force it. Because you do not."

He almost smiled at that, though the feeling behind it was not amusement. It was something like relief, the kind he felt when a colony accepted a change he had made and continued its work without distress.

He looked back out over the living basin.

"So," he said softly, "what's wrong with it?"

Saxifraga's gaze followed his. For a moment, her stillness deepened, as if she listened not only to the world before them but to the distance behind it, the unseen mechanisms, the buried lattice, the anchored presence of One-of-One holding the far side of the system steady.

"It is not wrong in the way humans mean it," she said at last.

Asa waited. He had learned that rushing a system—any system—only made it defensive.

"It endures," Saxifraga continued, "but it has begun to do so without answering itself. It is alive, but the exchanges that make life *more than survival* have narrowed."

Asa swallowed, the words landing somewhere he could feel them.

"Like a hive that's still working," he said slowly, "but stopped dancing."

Saxifraga's eyes shifted back to him. There was no surprise in her expression—only recognition, the way she had looked at him the first time she traced his frequency through the gate.

"Yes," she said. "Like that."

Asa breathed out.

He did not yet understand how lonely a world could be. Not truly. But standing at the threshold of the living basin, feeling the way the ground received him without fear, he thought he might learn.

Saxifraga stepped forward, not into the bog, but alongside it, following a line of growth where the surface changed texture—

firmer, patterned, as if the living had agreed to hold weight there.

"We will not begin with intervention," she said. "We will begin with listening."

Asa nodded.

"Show me how," he said.

Saxifraga did not answer with words. She lowered herself to one knee at the edge and placed her palm against the living surface with a gentleness that reminded Asa of the way he steadied a frame before removing comb.

The bog responded.

Not loudly. Not quickly.

But unmistakably.

A low harmonic passed through the ground and into Asa's bones—not sound exactly, not vibration. Timing.

Correspondence. A shared willingness to be present in the same field without forcing it.

Asa knelt beside her.

He did not press. He did not reach.

He simply laid his hand against the living ground and let his breath find the bog's slow rhythm.

For a long moment, nothing happened that could be pointed to. No light. No sign.

Then the world before them eased—only slightly—into a steadier coherence.

Saxifraga lifted her head, her expression unchanged, but something in her attention had softened.

"It is listening," she said.

Asa kept his hand where it was. "So are we."

Behind them, beyond distance, One-of-One registered the shift and sent its report across the span that no longer behaved as separation.

Listening sustained.

Withdrawal remains halted.

Continuation possible.

Saxifraga did not answer aloud. She did not need to.

Asa felt the weight of the moment settle into him, not a conclusion, not a rescue.

A beginning.

And somewhere in the living basin, beneath layers of growth that had endured without complaint, the bog breathed in and did not hesitate.

It held the breath.

As if waiting to learn what came next.

Chapter Two

What Endures

They did not enter the bog at once.

Saxifraga remained at the edge where the living surface firmed itself into something that could be stood upon without resistance. Asa stayed beside her, aware that the steadiness he felt was not an invitation to move faster, but permission to wait.

"The first error the builders made," Saxifraga said quietly, "was assuming endurance and continuity were the same."

Asa glanced at her. "They aren't."

"No," she agreed. "One survives. The other remembers."

They began by walking the perimeter.

The bog did not present borders in the way land did on Earth. There were no clear edges, no lines where one thing ended and another began. Instead, Asa learned to recognize shifts—

changes in texture beneath his boots, subtle variations in the

way moisture gathered, the way growth angled itself differently

depending on what lay beneath.

Saxifraga moved with certainty, though she did not hurry. At

times she paused without explanation, her attention extending

beyond sight. Asa learned to recognize those moments too.

When she stopped, something in the living basin was being

considered—not measured but *felt*.

"This region was once more active," she said at one such pause.

"Exchange between layers occurred more frequently here."

Asa knelt, resting his hand lightly against the surface. The bog

received contact without alteration.

"It's… quiet," he said.

"Yes," Saxifraga replied. "But not empty."

They moved inward.

Asa became aware of how little decay he saw. Growth layered upon itself, but it did not rot. Nothing collapsed inward. Nothing was reclaimed aggressively. The systems beneath—those ancient lattices Saxifraga had spoken of—continued to regulate moisture, nutrients, and balance.

"It's like a place that never gets sick," Asa said slowly, "but also never heals."

Saxifraga inclined her head. "That is an accurate distinction."

They reached a shallow depression where the surface thinned into something more fluid. Saxifraga stepped closer, careful not to disturb the pattern forming there. Asa followed her lead, watching rather than testing.

"This basin connects to the deeper circulation," she said. "Here, the bog once responded most clearly to itself."

"And now?" Asa asked.

Saxifraga did not answer immediately. Instead, she lowered herself again, placing her palm where the surface rippled faintly beneath her touch. Asa mirrored the motion beside her, aware now that imitation was not mimicry—it was alignment.

The bog answered them both.

Not with intensity, but with precision.

A faint correspondence passed between their contact points, a gentle synchronization that held for a moment and then eased. Asa felt it clearly this time: the bog was capable of response, but it did not *continue* the exchange.

"It answers," he said. "But it doesn't follow through."

"Yes," Saxifraga said. "It recognizes presence, but it does not sustain conversation."

Asa frowned, more thoughtful than troubled. "Like a hive that still senses vibration," he said, "but doesn't pass it on."

Saxifraga looked at him again, longer this time. "Your comparisons remain useful."

They rose and continued.

As the cycles passed—measured by the bog's slow rhythms rather than by time, Asa began to notice a pattern that had nothing to do with decay or imbalance. Everywhere they went, life was present. Everywhere, systems functioned. But nowhere did movement *between* living regions occur.

Each section of the bog existed complete unto itself.

"It's all compartmentalized," Asa said one cycle later, standing at a rise where the living surface thickened into something ridge-like. "Everything is doing its job. Nothing is carrying anything forward."

"That function once existed," Saxifraga said. "But it was never embedded. It depended on external life."

Asa looked at her. "Visitors."

"Participants," she corrected.

They traveled to the second bog through the fold, the transition now less strange to Asa. He no longer waited for sensation. He waited for correspondence.

This bog lay beneath a dimmer sky. Its basin was broader, its growth patterns more diffuse. It appeared healthier—more movement, more variation. But the longer Asa observed, the clearer the similarity became.

It endured.

It did not adapt.

A third bog revealed the same truth, though expressed differently. Here, growth surged in cycles, then stalled, as if the world periodically remembered how to reach outward and then forgot why it should.

"They all feel…" Asa searched for the word. "Self-contained."

"Yes," Saxifraga said. "That was once considered a strength."

Asa shook his head slowly. "Not for living things."

They stood together at the edge of the third basin, the light shifting across surfaces that breathed without urgency.

"These worlds aren't broken," Asa said. "They're isolated."

Saxifraga felt the truth of it settle through her awareness. It aligned with what she had measured, what One-of-One had confirmed, what the systems could never quite articulate.

"They were designed to persist," she said. "Not to relate."

Asa looked out over the bog, then down at his own hands. He flexed his fingers once, feeling the steadiness there, the learned restraint that had shaped him.

"Life doesn't work like that," he said quietly. "Not the kind that lasts."

Saxifraga followed his gaze.

"No," she agreed. "It does not."

They did not speak again for a long while.

The bogs breathed on. The systems endured. And somewhere between the living surfaces and the silence that threaded them, a truth was beginning to take shape—one neither of them would rush to name.

But it was there.

Waiting.

Chapter Three

The Pattern Between

They returned to the first bog with a unique way of seeing.

Nothing in the basin had changed during their absence—not in form, not in function. The living surface still layered itself with patient regularity. Moisture still rose and settled. The lattice beneath continued its quiet work without error.

And yet, Asa felt the difference immediately.

"It's quieter," he said.

Saxifraga paused beside him. "It has not withdrawn further."

"No," Asa agreed. "But it's waiting."

They stood together, neither entering nor retreating, allowing the steadiness to declare itself. Asa had learned by now that waiting was not in action. It was an active refusal to impose.

Saxifraga extended her awareness into the deeper systems, not to interrogate them, but to confirm what they already knew. The report returned unchanged.

Stability sustained.

No degradation detected.

No expansion initiated.

Endurance, without momentum.

Asa crouched and traced a line in the living surface with one finger, careful not to disturb the structure beneath. The bog did not recoil. It accepted the contact and then let it go.

"Everything here is connected," he said slowly, "but nothing *travels*."

Saxifraga inclined her head. "Clarify."

"In the hives," Asa said, "no single part knows the whole. But everything moves—nectar, pollen, signal, heat. If that

movement stops, the hive does not die right away. It just…
closes in on itself."

He looked up at her. "That's what this feels like."

Saxifraga considered the comparison. She overlaid it against records from other worlds, other failures, other recoveries. The alignment was precise.

"This system was designed to minimize loss," she said. "Movement was considered inefficiency."

Asa let out a quiet breath. "Movement is how life remembers there's more than one place to be."

They walked deeper into the basin.

Asa noticed now that the bog's response to him, though real, was localized. Where he stepped, coherence sharpened. Where he knelt, growth oriented. But as soon as he moved on, the effect softened, dispersing rather than propagating.

"It doesn't follow me," he said. "It lets me pass."

"Yes," Saxifraga said. "It recognizes you, but it does not yet understand what to do with that recognition."

Asa straightened, looking out over the basin. "Because it doesn't know how to carry it forward."

They stopped near a region where the surface thinned again, opening into a shallow flow. Saxifraga knelt, and Asa followed.

"Tell me something," Asa said. "When these worlds were new—before the builders left—what moved between them?"

Saxifraga's stillness deepened. She searched for old records, not stored in language but in resonance patterns preserved across time.

"Life," she said at last. "Not seeded. Not transported. Drawn."

Asa waited.

"Creatures that crossed thresholds without altering them," she continued. "They did not belong to any single world. They moved between systems as part of their own cycles."

Asa felt something settle into place behind his eyes—not a conclusion, but a narrowing of uncertainty.

"Pollinators," he said quietly.

Saxifraga turned toward him.

"Yes," she said. "Though not as your world defines them. The function preceded the form."

Asa nodded. "On Earth, that kind of life does not stay put. It carries what one place has learned to another place that is ready to receive it."

He looked down at his hands again, suddenly aware of memory rising without effort—the weight of a frame, the sound of wings, the way a hive changed when something new was introduced gently.

"They don't just move pollen," he said. "They move *permission*."

Saxifraga did not interrupt.

"They don't fix the plant," Asa continued. "They do not tell it how to grow. They just show up, over and over, until the plant remembers it can change."

The bog breathed beneath them.

Saxifraga felt the truth of it rippled through her awareness—not as data, but as recognition. The builders accounted for structure, balance, and endurance.

They had not accounted for companionship.

"These worlds were never meant to be closed systems," she said.

"No," Asa agreed. "They were meant to be visited."

They sat together in the living basin, neither moving nor withdrawing. The pattern between them—human, guardian, world—settled into a new configuration.

No solution.

Direction.

Saxifraga lifted her gaze toward the dim sky. Somewhere beyond it, across distances that no longer behaved as separation, the network of dormant gates held itself in listening readiness.

"The next step," she said, "is to confirm."

Asa nodded. "We need to see if every bog is missing the same thing."

"Yes."

"And if they are?"

Saxifraga did not answer at once.

Then, quietly, "Then we must decide whether life can be invited to return."

Asa closed his eyes for a moment, feeling the steadiness, he carried, the memory of wings and movement and exchange.

"Life doesn't go where it's taken," he said. "It goes where it's welcomed."

Saxifraga felt the alignment held.

The bog did not surge. It did not respond with urgency or demand.

But beneath the living surface, something ancient and patient shifted its attention subtle as breath, unmistakable as readiness.

The pattern between worlds had been named.

What remained was to learn whether it could be sown.

Chapter Four

The Same Silence

They confirmed it by going where the answer could not hide.

The next bog lay farther from the original basin, reached through a gate that listened weakly at first and then steadied as Saxifraga adjusted her approach. Asa felt the transition before he understood it—not as movement, but as a change in how the world received him.

This place breathed more slowly.

The basin spread wide beneath a dimmer sky, its living surface stretched thin, its growth patterns elongated as if the world had learned to conserve rather than respond. At a distance it appeared active—ripples of motion, subtle shifts of color—but when Asa stepped closer, the familiar quiet settled in.

Not emptiness.

Absence.

"It's doing the same thing," Asa said after only a few moments.

Saxifraga agreed. She knelt, placed her palm against the surface, and waited. The bog answered—precisely, politely—and then withdrew from the exchange without continuing it.

Endurance without reply.

They moved deeper.

Here, the systems were more visible to Saxifraga's perception. The lattice beneath the living layers pulsed at regular intervals, regulating moisture and nutrient flow with impeccable precision. No fault registered. No imbalance escalated. The world was, by every measurable standard, healthy.

And yet Asa felt no invitation.

"It's like walking into a room where everyone's awake," he said quietly, "but no one's talking."

Saxifraga inclined her head. "Yes."

They visited another basin after that, and another.

Some were younger, their growth still flexible, their living surfaces more responsive. Others had endured for so long that their patterns had settled into repetition, repeating success without variation. But the conditions remained consistent.

Recognition without continuation.

Response without exchange.

Life without movement between lives.

By the time they reached the fifth bog, Asa no longer needed to touch the ground to feel it. He sensed the silence in the way the world held itself—careful, complete, and inward.

"They're all like this," he said.

"Yes," Saxifraga replied. "The variance lies only in degree."

They stood at the edge of that basin, the living surface breathing slowly below them.

"This isn't decay," Asa said. "And it's not damage."

"No."

"It's loneliness," he said.

The word did not echo. It did not resonate dramatically.

It simply fits.

Saxifraga felt something shift within her awareness—not surprise, but release. The records she carried, the measurements she had taken, the patterns she had traced across worlds aligned cleanly around the word Asa had chosen.

"Yes," she said at last. "That is the condition."

Asa frowned slightly, not in confusion, but in care. "Worlds aren't supposed to be alone."

"No," Saxifraga agreed. "They are meant to be in conversation."

They remained there, letting the truth settle without forcing implication.

Finally, Asa spoke again. "When the builders were here—before they left—these places had visitors."

"They did," Saxifraga said. "Life that moved freely between systems. Not bound to one world. Not owned."

"And when that movement stopped," Asa said, "the worlds didn't break."

"No."

"They just… closed."

"Yes."

Asa looked out over the basin. "That's why the systems can't fix this."

Saxifraga followed his reasoning easily. "Systems maintain. They do not accompany."

Asa let out a slow breath. "Life accompanies life."

The bog breathed beneath them, unchanged by the conclusion yet subtly attentive to it.

Saxifraga felt One-of-One register the accumulated data across distance.

Condition confirmed across surveyed basins, it reported. Longevity sustained.
Relational exchange absent.

Saxifraga inclined her head slightly. "We see it."

The report continued.

Projected outcome without intervention:
Persistent isolation.

Gradual narrowing of variance.

Eventual irreversible stillness.

Asa did not need the projection explained. He had seen hives reach that state—not dead, not collapsed, but closed so tightly around themselves that nothing new could enter.

"What brings it back?" he asked quietly.

Saxifraga did not answer at once.

She looked instead at Asa—at the way, the living fields around him held steady without tension, at the way each world had responded to his presence without fear or resistance.

"Movement," she said. "But not invasion."

Asa nodded. "Life that goes back and forth."

"Yes."

"Carrying what one place learns into another," he added.

"Yes."

They stood together, the answer forming between them not as revelation, but as inevitability.

Asa closed his eyes briefly, and memory rose without effort: the hum of wings, the weight of a hive in balance, the way a field changed after something small and living had passed through it.

He opened his eyes.

"I think I know what kind of life this needs," he said.

Saxifraga did not rush him.

"Not something that stays," Asa continued. "Something that moves. Something that does not belong to just one place."

Saxifraga felt the alignment tighten—not with urgency, but with clarity.

"Yes," she said softly.

Asa looked down at his hands again.

"On Earth," he said, "that kind of life is not loud. Most people do not notice it until it is gone."

The bog beneath them did not react.

But across the network, a dormant gate shifted—so slightly that no instrument would have marked it.

Listening had deepened.

The silence they had found was no longer empty.

It was waiting.

Chapter Five

What Moves Between

They did not speak the name at first.

Asa felt it forming long before the word rose—an understanding shaped by memory rather than logic. He had learned, tending the hives, that naming something too soon could narrow it, turn a living relationship into a fixed idea. This was not a thing to be fixed.

It was a function.

They returned again to the first bog, not to confirm what they already knew, but to watch more closely now that the pattern had revealed itself. Saxifraga adjusted nothing. She allowed the world to show them what it would.

Asa walked slowly, stopping where the surface accepted him most readily. He knelt where the growth shifted orientation at his presence, where moisture gathered in subtle spirals rather than pooling. He did not touch at first. He watched.

"The response follows you," Saxifraga observed.

"Yes," Asa said. "But it doesn't travel past me."

Saxifraga inclined her head. "You are a point, not a pathway."

Asa considered that. "That's the problem."

He placed his palm lightly against the living surface again. The bog answered—steady, precise—and then held. No further signal passed outward. No echo carried to the edges of the basin.

"It's like bringing one bee into a field," Asa said quietly. "The flower responds. The field does not change."

Saxifraga's attention sharpened. "Clarify."

"One bee can touch a plant," Asa said. "But pollination is not touch. It is movement. Back and forth. Over and over. Between places."

Saxifraga felt the truth of it ripple through her awareness. The builders' designs had allowed for presence, even exchange—but never circulation.

"They built worlds," she said slowly, "that could endure without visitors."

"And forgot that visitors are how worlds *stay alive*," Asa replied.

They moved to another basin, then another. Asa repeated the same simple action in each place—kneeling, touching, waiting. The response was always the same.

Recognition.

Acceptance.

No propagation.

The bogs could listen.

They could not yet *speak to one another*.

Asa straightened from the last basin and looked across the living surface, his brow furrowed not with frustration, but with care.

"This isn't something you can teach a world," he said. "It has to be practiced."

"Yes," Saxifraga said. "Repeatedly."

"By life that doesn't stay put."

Saxifraga turned her attention inward, consulting the deeper records—the remnants of pathways once active across the network. Faint traces emerged: routes that had never been designed for transport of matter alone, but for return.

"They were not conduits," she said. "They were cycles."

Asa smiled faintly. "That sounds right."

He walked a few paces farther into the basin, then stopped. The steadiness he carried shifted—subtly, unmistakably, into memory.

"I didn't teach the bees to do what they do," he said. "I learned by watching them. They do not move because they are told. They move because something calls to them, and something else answers."

Saxifraga watched him closely now.

"And when that movement stops?" she asked.

"The whole system tightens," Asa said. "Not at once. Slowly. Quietly."

The bog breathed beneath them, unchanged yet attentive.

Saxifraga felt the realization settle fully at last—not as discovery, but as confirmation of something the worlds themselves had been waiting to have named.

"These bogs are not incomplete," she said. "They are unfinished."

Asa nodded. "They were meant to grow together."

Silence followed—not the absence of sound, but the kind that came when a living system adjusted to the truth it recognized.

Finally, Saxifraga spoke again. "If we are correct, then one world alone cannot restore what has been lost."

Asa did not hesitate. "No. It would need to be shared."

"And if the life that shares it is removed from its origin?" she asked.

Asa looked at her steadily. "Then it has to go willingly."

Saxifraga felt the weight of that settle between them.

"We cannot take," she said.

"No," Asa agreed. "And we can't rush."

They stood together at the edge of the basin, the living surface stretching out before them—alive, patient, incomplete.

Asa exhaled slowly.

"I think it's time we go back," he said.

Saxifraga did not ask why. She already felt the shift in the field, the way the network's listening had tightened, the way distant gates had begun to adjust their attention toward a world that still practiced movement without ownership.

"Yes," she said. "Not to bring an answer."

Asa glanced at her. "To ask a question."

The bog did not resist the thought.

Across the living basins, subtle correspondences stirred—not opening, not awakening—but aligning themselves to a possibility that had not existed before.

For the first time since the builders had departed, the worlds were not merely enduring.

They were preparing.

And far away, on Earth, a hive stirred—

not in alarm,

but in recognition.

Chapter Six

The Question of Return

They did not leave immediately.

That, too, mattered.

Saxifraga felt the network settle into a state she had not measured before—not dormant, not active, but *held*. The gates no longer listened outward indiscriminately. Their attention had narrowed, aligning toward a single probability that had not yet resolved.   "Readiness without demand."

The ship did not return when they did.

It remained held in listening orbit—not as a vessel, but as an anchor. Its purpose had shifted the moment Asa crossed the fold. What had once carried a traveler now carried coherence, stabilizing the corridor between worlds without forcing it open.

The passage no longer depended on activation. It depended on use—measured, willing, and able to return.

"You could go alone," he said at last.

Saxifraga turned toward him. "Yes."

"And you won't," Asa added.

"No."

They stood at the edge of the basin, the living surface breathing slowly before them. The bog no longer leaned inward at Asa's presence. It held itself, as if aware that what it needed could not be given here.

"It matters how we leave," Asa said.

"Yes," Saxifraga agreed. "If we depart as extraction, the field will narrow again."

Asa nodded. "And if we leave as invitation?"

Saxifraga considered the phrasing carefully. "Then the path remains open."

They returned through the fold with the same restraint that had marked their arrival. Asa no longer searched for sensation. He let the transition complete itself in its own way.

Earth received him like a held note resolving—not with relief, but with continuity.

The clearing was unchanged. The stones stood where they had stood. The forest moved as it always had. Birds resumed their calls without pause.

And yet Asa felt it at once.

The hives were awake.

Not agitated. Not disturbed.

Aware.

He did not hurry toward them. He had learned that haste unsettled what needed space. Instead, he walked the familiar path, feeling the ground meet him with the same steadiness it always had—only now, that steadiness extended beyond the land beneath his feet.

Saxifraga followed at a respectful distance, her presence unmarked by disruption. The forest accepted her as it had before, branches parting without resistance, insects resuming their patterns as soon as she passed.

Asa stopped at the edge of the apiary.

The bees moved differently.

Their flight paths overlapped more closely than usual, arcs tightening and widening in patterns that reminded him of alignment rather than work. The sound of the hives was not louder.

It was fuller.

"They feel it," he said.

"Yes," Saxifraga replied. "Their cycles are sensitive to coherence."

Asa stepped closer and rested his hand lightly against the nearest box. The colony did not surge. It settled.

He closed his eyes.

The steadiness within him widened again—not outward this time, but downward, threading through memory and presence alike. He felt the hives as he always had not as possession, not as obligation, but as relationship.

Then something new emerged.

Not a pull.

A question.

Asa opened his eyes and looked back at Saxifraga. "They're not asking to go," he said slowly.

Saxifraga waited.

"They're asking *where*," he finished.

Saxifraga felt the distinction settle into the field like a careful placement of weight. "That is correct," she said. "They cannot be taken. They must be welcomed."

Asa nodded. "And not all of them."

"No," Saxifraga agreed. "Continuity requires return."

Asa exhaled slowly. "Then we start small."

They did not open the hives that day.

Instead, Asa moved among them, adjusting frames, redistributing weight, preparing—not for departure, but for choice. Saxifraga observed in silence, learning how preparation looked in a system that could not be commanded.

As evening settled, Asa stepped back and studied the apiary as a whole.

"Not all flowers are ready at the same time," he said. "And not every bee goes on every flight."

Saxifraga inclined her head. "That principle applies across systems."

Asa smiled faintly. "Good. Because this is not about saving anything."

"No," Saxifraga agreed. "It is about beginning again."

They stood together as the light faded, the hives humming softly behind them, not restless, not disturbed.

Listening.

The question had been asked.

The answer, when it came, would not arrive at all at once.

And across distance that no longer behaved as separation, the bogs held their breath—not in need, not in fear—

but in expectation of company.

Chapter Seven

What May Be Carried

The choice did not come as a single moment.

Asa had learned long ago that the most important decisions in a living system rarely announced themselves. They emerged through small confirmation patterns holding steady, responses repeating without strain, the absence of resistance where resistance had once been expected.

He spent the next cycle as he always had.

He rose with the light. He walked the perimeter. He listened to the hives before he opened them, letting their tone tell him more than motion ever could. Saxifraga remained nearby, never intruding, her attention broad and patient, learning how a system guided itself without instruction.

The bees responded to her presence without alarm.

That alone mattered.

"They don't see you as outside," Asa observed one morning.

Saxifraga inclined her head slightly. "Nor do they see themselves as separate."

Asa smiled at that. "That's about right."

He opened the first hive slowly, lifting the lid just enough to let air and attention pass between inside and out. The bees continued their work, adjusting only by degree. He leaned close, breathing evenly, letting the rhythm settle into him.

He felt it then—not a command, not an urge.

Readiness.

Not all of them.

Not yet.

Asa closed the hive again and stepped back.

"They're not resisting," he said. "But they're not finished here."

Saxifraga listened, not to his words alone, but to the way the field held around them. "Then we do not hurry."

They moved among the hives for several cycles more, Asa making small adjustments—spacing frames, redistributing weight, marking which colonies responded most readily to change. He did not isolate them. He let them remain part of the whole.

"It's not about which bees are strongest," he said one evening. "It's about which ones already move between without trouble."

Saxifraga followed his attention. "Carriers."

"Yes."

He paused at one hive in particular. The sound there was different, not louder, not sharper. More fluid. Movement overlapped without collision. The bees within responded to change as if they had been waiting for it.

"This one," Asa said quietly.

Saxifraga did not question him.

They prepared the transport without removing anything yet.

Not cages.

Not containment.

Instead, Saxifraga adapted the fold—not as passage for mass, but as *continuation*. She did not compress space. She aligned it, creating a corridor that would allow return without rupture.

Asa watched her work closely.

"You're not opening it," he said.

"No," she replied. "I am allowing it to be acknowledged."

Asa nodded. "That's how the bees do it too."

The night before the crossing, Asa sat alone near the hives. He did not wear protection. He did not need it. The bees moved around him without agitation, some landing briefly on his hands, others passing close without contact.

He spoke softly, not in language, but in presence.

He did not tell them where they would go.

He let them feel it.

The bog answered faintly across distance, not calling, not pulling—only offering space.

Asa felt the response ripple through the colonies like a question moving wing to wing.

In the morning, the answer arrived.

Not as agreement.

As willingness.

Only a portion of the hive shifted its pattern, movement aligning subtly toward the prepared threshold. The rest continued their work unchanged.

Asa let out a breath he had not realized he was holding.

"That's enough," he said.

"Yes," Saxifraga agreed. "More would be harm."

They opened the passage at dawn.

Not wide.

Not dramatic.

The fold did not tear the air. It curved it gently, aligning Earth's field with the bog's receptive basin. The bees did not rush. They did not swarm.

They moved.

Wing by wing.

Arc by arc.

Each one crossed as if following a familiar route that had simply been extended.

Asa stood beside the opening, steady and present. He did not guide them. He did not count.

He trusted the pattern.

Saxifraga watched the field shift—not destabilize but deepen. The corridor held without strain. Earth did not thin behind them. The bog did not overwhelm what entered.

This was not transport.

It was exchange.

When the last of the carriers crossed, the fold settled back into stillness on its own. The hives remained alive, active, whole.

Continuity preserved.

Asa exhaled slowly.

"Now," he said.

"Yes," Saxifraga replied. "Now we listen."

Far away, in the living basin, the first carriers entered the bog's field.

Not as invaders.

Not as saviors.

As life that knew how to move between life.

The bog did not surge.

It did not brighten or bloom.

It adjusted.

Across the surface, growth patterns loosened, no longer tightening inward. Exchange began—not dramatic, not fast— but unmistakable.

For the first time since the builders had left, something moved *through* the world rather than upon it.

And the bog did not hesitate.

It welcomed them.

Chapter Eight

The First Return

The bog did not respond at once.

Saxifraga had expected that. Restoration, when it came honestly, never arrived as display. It came as permission—slight changes that accumulated until they altered the whole.

Asa felt the shift before he saw anything move.

The air above the living basin held differently now. Not heavier. Not brighter. *Layered.* As if something that had once passed through and never returned had learned the shape of the place and decided to stay—briefly, carefully, without possession.

The bees moved low at first.

They did not scatter across the basin. They followed lines of growth that already existed, tracing routes the bog seemed prepared to show them. Their wings stirred no alarm. The living surface beneath them did not recoil.

It opened.

Not visibly. Not structurally. But in attention.

Asa stood at the edge, hands at his sides, resisting the instinct to step closer. This was not his work to guide. It was his work to *allow*.

"They're not changing it," he said quietly.

"No," Saxifraga replied. "They are reminding it."

The first carrier touched down on a flowering node near the basin's center. The structure there had existed before—stable, self-contained, quietly productive. When the bee landed, nothing dramatic occurred.

But the exchange did not end when the bee lifted away.

The node held the contact.

Moisture shifted. Nutrient flow altered by a fraction too small for any instrument to isolate. Nearby growth adjusted orientation—not toward the bee, but toward *each other*.

Asa's breath caught—not in excitement, but in recognition.

"That's it," he said softly. "That's the part that was missing."

Saxifraga extended her awareness through the basin. The resonance that had once thinned now traveled—not broadly, not forcefully—but *between*. Signals passed laterally. The bog's internal exchanges widened without strain.

The world was no longer speaking only to itself.

One-of-One registered the change across distance.

Exchange propagation detected, it reported.

No instability observed.

Variance increasing within sustainable thresholds.

"Yes," Saxifraga said. "That is how it should begin."

The bees continued their movement, never lingering too long in one place. They crossed from node to node, basin to basin, carrying nothing that could be named and everything that mattered.

Asa watched them work.

"They don't know they're fixing anything," he said.

Saxifraga inclined her head. "They are not fixing. They are participating."

The bog responded slowly.

Not by growth alone, but by *memory*. Patterns that had existed in isolation now overlapped. Regions that had once held their coherence tightly began to share it. The living surface did not become more active.

It became more *aware*.

Asa stepped forward then, just a pace, careful not to intrude. He knelt and placed his hand against the ground again.

This time, the response did not stop at his palm.

The correspondence passed through him and continued outward, following the paths the bees had begun to trace. Asa felt it moved away from him without loss, as if something he had carried for years had finally learned how to travel on its own.

He laughed once, quietly.

Saxifraga turned toward him. "What is it?"

"I'm not the bridge anymore," he said. "I'm just part of the traffic."

Saxifraga felt the truth of that settle into her awareness. The burden she had carried since awakening—the fear that continuity depended too heavily on one presence—eased.

This world would not survive by guardianship alone.

It would survive by relationship.

The bees returned to the corridor at intervals, crossing back toward Earth as naturally as they had come. Some remained longer. Some left sooner. None were trapped.

Continuity preserved.

Saxifraga observed the fold settle into a stable cycle rather than a fixed opening. The passage no longer waited to be activated.

It waited to be *used*.

"This will not be the only world," she said.

Asa nodded. "They'll figure that out."

"They already have," Saxifraga replied.

Across the basin, the living surface stirred—not dramatically, not urgently—but with a new kind of patience. The bog breathed, and this time, the breath did not fall back into itself.

It traveled.

What had been lonely was no longer alone.

And for the first time since the builders had departed, the worlds were not merely holding their shape.

They were learning how to share it.

Chapter Nine

What Begins to Travel

The change did not announce itself.

That, Saxifraga realized, was the surest sign that it was real.

The bog did not brighten or surge with growth. Its surface did not erupt into color or movement. What altered was subtler, more profound—the *timing* of things. Where cycles had once repeated in isolation, they now overlapped. Where responses had ended at their point of origin, they continued.

Movement had learned how to return.

Asa noticed it first at the edges.

He stood at a rise overlooking the basin, watching the bees trace their quiet paths. Their routes no longer followed only the most receptive nodes. They crossed into regions that had once felt closed, their presence neither resisted nor absorbed too quickly. The bog did not simply accept them.

It answered them.

"Look," Asa said softly.

Saxifraga followed his attention. At the basin's perimeter, growth that had long remained static shifted orientation—not directly toward the bees, but toward pathways the bees had already passed through. Exchange no longer depended on constant contact.

The bog was learning.

"This is propagation," Saxifraga said. "Not repair."

Asa nodded. "That is how it spreads on Earth too. You do not keep replanting the same flower. You let the field teach itself."

The bees began to move beyond the first basin.

Not all at once. Not in a swarm.

One by one, small groups followed the fold's gentle curvature toward neighboring bogs. The corridor did not widen to accommodate them. It adjusted its attention, aligning with the bees' timing rather than demanding its own.

Saxifraga felt the shift ripple through the network.

Second basin receiving exchange, One-of-One reported. No destabilization detected.

Asa let out a breath he had not realized he was holding.

"They're doing it on their own," he said.

"Yes," Saxifraga replied. "Which means we no longer control the outcome."

Asa smiled faintly. "Good."

They followed the movement to the second bog, arriving not as initiators but as witnesses. The basin there responded differently than the first. Its growth patterns loosened more slowly, its internal exchanges cautious, as if testing the safety of this new conversation.

The bees did not press.

They moved briefly, touching only what responded willingly, then departed again. Nothing was forced.

"It's like introducing a neighbor," Asa said. "You do not rearrange the house. You just open the door."

Saxifraga felt the resonance stabilize further. The network no longer held itself narrowly around the original basin. It widened—not outward, but *between.*

Across distance, dormant gates shifted their orientation slightly, no longer listening only for command or activation.

They listened for *return.*

One-of-One's reports grew quieter.

Monitoring sufficient, it transmitted.

System intervention no longer primary.

Saxifraga accepted the change without resistance. She had been placed to observe thresholds, not to occupy them forever.

Asa watched the bees vanish into the fold and return again, their cycles expanding naturally.

"They'll need places to rest," he said after a while.

"Yes," Saxifraga agreed. "And the worlds will need to learn how to host."

Asa glanced at her. "That means this isn't finished."

"No," she replied. "It has only become self-sustaining."

They stood together as the bog breathed beneath them, its rhythm now layered with new timing. The loneliness they had traced across worlds did not vanish completely.

But it no longer defined the system.

What moved between the bogs carried more than exchange. It carried *expectation*. Not of rescue. Not of completion.

Of continuation.

Asa rested his hands at his sides, feeling the steadiness within him ease into something lighter.

"I used to think tending meant staying in one place," he said.

Saxifraga turned toward him. "And now?"

"Now I think it means making sure nothing has to stay alone."

The bog answered—not with words, not with signs—but with a deepening coherence that no longer required his presence to hold.

Across the living basins, something ancient and patient adjusted its posture.

The age of isolation was ending.

What had been sown was beginning to travel.

Chapter Ten

The Work That Remains

The world did not need them in the same way anymore.

Saxifraga felt that truth settle slowly, the way stone accepted warmth after a long cold. It was not dismissal. It was graduation—from singular guardianship to shared tending.

The bogs continued their exchange without instruction.

Bees moved through the fold in measured cycles, some returning to Earth, others lingering longer among the living basins. The passage no longer felt like a threshold that required attention. It behaved like a path worn gently enough that it never scared the ground.

Asa watched the rhythm establish itself.

"They're setting their own limits," he said.

"Yes," Saxifraga replied. "Life rarely exceeds what it can return from."

They traveled again—not to intervene, but to observe.

In one bog, growth thickened in unfamiliar places, not spreading outward aggressively but folding inward toward overlap. In another, regions that had once repeated the same cycle without variation began to differentiate subtly, learning distinction without separation.

"These places are learning how to *host*," Asa said.

"Yes," Saxifraga agreed. "And how to release."

He smiled faintly. "That's harder."

They stood at the edge of a basin where the surface rose into delicate arches—structures that had existed before but had never connected. Now thin filaments bridged the spaces between them, not solid, not permanent, but present enough to allow exchange.

Asa knelt and touched one lightly.

The structure did not collapse.

It responded.

He drew his hand back, letting the contact end cleanly.

"That's new," he said.

Saxifraga extended her awareness, tracing the change across the basin and into the deeper lattice. The systems beneath had not been altered.

They had been *relieved*.

"Systems were built to compensate," she said slowly. "They are now being allowed to rest."

Asa exhaled. "That is good. Nothing should hold everything forever."

Saxifraga felt One-of-One registered the same realization across distance.

Load redistribution confirmed, it reported.

Sustained balance no longer singularly dependent.

Saxifraga inclined her head slightly. "You may reduce oversight."

Acknowledged.

The exchange ended without ceremony.

Asa looked at her then—not as the one who had brought him here, but as a fellow witness to something larger than either of them.

"What happens now?" he asked.

Saxifraga did not answer immediately. She considered the question as she always had—by listening to what did not demand response.

"The builders will not return," she said at last. "Not as they were."

Asa nodded. "They wouldn't recognize this."

"No," she agreed. "Nor should they."

They walked together along a path the bog had formed naturally—firm enough to hold, flexible enough to change. Asa noticed how easily his steps fit now, how the world no longer adjusted sharply to his presence.

He was not the anomaly anymore.

He was part of the pattern.

"There will be other worlds," Asa said. "Other places like this."

"Yes," Saxifraga replied. "And not all will be ready."

Asa stopped walking. "Then we don't rush."

"No."

"We don't bring life where it can't return," he said.

"No."

"And we don't stay where we're no longer needed."

Saxifraga turned toward him. "That, too, is part of stewardship."

They stood together as the bog breathed around them, no longer waiting, no longer withdrawing.

The work had changed.

What remained was not fixing or guarding but *tending the spaces between*—watching for imbalance not of structure, but of relationship.

Asa felt the steadiness within him settle into something lighter still.

"I think," he said quietly, "this is what sowing really means."

Saxifraga inclined her head. "Yes."

They did not mark the moment.

The worlds did that for them—by continuing.

And in the quiet movement of bees between Earth and basin,

between flower and living surface, between what had been

alone and what now remembered how to share—

the future did not arrive at all at once.

It began, as it always had,

with care.

Chapter Eleven

The World That Hesitated

Not all worlds answered the same way.

Saxifraga sensed the difference before they emerged. The fold tightened—not in resistance, but in caution, as if the destination were weighing the cost of attention before allowing itself to be known.

"This one is listening," she said quietly. "But it is uncertain."

Asa nodded. "So, we don't rush."

They stepped out onto stone that had once been deliberately shaped and then left to weather back into the land. The basin beyond was smaller than the others, its living surface compact, its rhythms tightly held. Where the earlier bogs had opened slowly to exchange, this one held itself close.

The bees did not enter at once.

They hovered near the threshold, wings tracing careful arcs, testing the air without committing to it. Asa felt the pause ripple through the field—not fear, but memory.

"This world's been interrupted before," he said.

"Yes," Saxifraga replied. "Its exchanges were once forced."

They waited.

Minutes passed. Then longer intervals, measured not by time but by steadiness. Asa stood still, breathing evenly, letting the alignment within him remain open without persistence.

At last, a single carrier crossed.

The bog did not recoil—but neither did it answer.

The bee lingered briefly, touched nothing, then returned through the fold.

Asa exhaled. "That's okay."

Saxifraga turned to him. "You are certain?"

"Yes," he said. "It heard the question. It just is nct ready to answer."

They withdrew without disappointment.

Behind them, the hesitant world remained intact—not diminished by refusal, not pressured by expectation.

"These matters," Saxifraga said as they returned to the fold.

Asa nodded. "It means we're not imposing."

Chapter Twelve

Consequence Without Collapse

The network adjusted.

Saxifraga felt it across the listening gates—a redistribution of attention rather than a surge of activation. Worlds that had accepted exchange stabilized further. Worlds that hesitated were not bypassed.

They were *remembered*.

One-of-One confirmed the change.

Adaptive response detected.
Network coherence increasing without uniformity.

"That's new," Asa said.

"Yes," Saxifraga replied. "Uniformity was once mistaken for success."

They returned to Earth briefly—not to intervene, but to confirm continuity. The hives remained balanced. The bees that had stayed behind carried on without disruption. Those that traveled returned when their cycles completed, reintegrating seamlessly.

Movement had broken nothing.

"That's the proof," Asa said. "If it didn't return cleanly, it wouldn't last."

Saxifraga felt the relief she had not allowed herself since awakening.

For the first time, the fate of the bogs did not rest on her vigilance alone.

Chapter Thirteen

The Shape of Stewardship

They no longer traveled constantly.

That, too, was part of learning.

Saxifraga remained near the first basin, observing how the exchange sustained itself without guidance. Asa moved between Earth and the network as needed, not as messenger or guardian, but as *listener*—noting when movement slowed, when attention narrowed, when rest was required.

Stewardship revealed itself not as action, but as restraint.

"You know," Asa said one cycle, watching the bees trace their quiet routes, "people think tending is about keeping things going."

Saxifraga waited.

"But most of the time," he continued, "it's about knowing when to stop."

"Yes," she said. "And when to trust."

They watched as a second hesitant world opened slightly—not enough for exchange, but enough to acknowledge presence. The bees hovered near it, respectful, patient.

No one crossed.

And that was enough.

Chapter Fourteen

What Will Not Be Rebuilt

A message arrived at last.

Not in words.

In pattern.

One-of-One received it first, its ancient awareness attuned to the
deep signatures of the builders who had once departed.

Origin confirmed, it reported.
Intent: observation only.

"They are watching," Saxifraga said.

Asa did not look troubled. "They don't get to decide anymore."

"No," she agreed. "They chose endurance over relationship.
This is what followed."

The message carried no demand, no claim.

Only recognition.

The builders would not return to reclaim their systems.

They would not rebuild what no longer needed them.

That, Saxifraga realized, was the final consequence of choosing restraint over control.

Chapter Fifteen

The Work That Continues

The bogs breathed on.

Some exchanged freely now, their rhythms layered and resilient. Others remained quiet, holding themselves until readiness arrived. None collapsed. None surged beyond their capacity.

Life had been reintroduced without dominance.

Asa stood beside Saxifraga at the basin's edge, the living surface before them no longer lonely, no longer closed.

"We didn't save them," he said.

"No," she replied. "We accompanied them."

He smiled faintly. "That feels right."

Saxifraga felt the same.

The era of seeking had ended.

The era of sowing had begun.

What followed would not be dramatic.

It would be durable.

And across worlds once isolated by their own success, life

moved—quietly, patiently—between life again.

Not because it was commanded.

But because it was welcome.

Chapter Sixteen

The World That Answered

The final bog did not hesitate.

Saxifraga felt the difference the moment the fold began to loosen—not a rush forward, not eagerness, but readiness held with care. The alignment did not tighten into focus; it widened, as though the world ahead had already made room.

"This one remembers," she said softly.

Asa nodded. "Or it's been waiting."

They emerged beneath a sky that carried more light than the others, not brighter, but steadier, as if the atmosphere itself had learned how to hold illumination without glare. The basin before them spread in gentle terraces, each layer breathing in time with the next. Growth did not cluster inward here. It reached—carefully, deliberately—across space.

The bees crossed the threshold without pause.

Not all of them. Just enough.

They moved low and slow, wings tracing patient arcs that followed existing lines of life. The bog responded immediately—not with change, but with recognition. Exchange did not need to be taught here.

It resumed.

Asa felt it passing through him like a long-held breath released. The steadiness he carried loosened into something lighter, freer.

"They don't need us," he said quietly.

Saxifraga watched the living surface adjust—growth bridging terraces, moisture redistributing, cycles overlapping without strain. "No," she agreed. "They needed confirmation."

They stayed only long enough to be certain.

Then they withdrew.

This world did not require witnessing.

It would continue on its own.

Chapter Seventeen

The Measure of Enough

They returned to the first basin where everything had begun.

The bog there was no longer the same—not because it had been altered beyond recognition, but because it now carried *history*. Exchange moved through it in layers, traces of contact lingering long enough to matter and then passing on without accumulation.

Saxifraga stood at the edge and felt no pull to intervene.

That, she realized, was the measure of enough.

One-of-One transmitted a final assessment.

Network stability sustained.

Relational exchange embedded.

Guardian intervention no longer primary.

Saxifraga inclined her head. "Acknowledged."

The response came without ceremony.

Asa watched her, sensing the quiet finality of the moment.

"That was your job," he said.

"Yes," she replied. "And now it is not."

He smiled faintly. "That happens more often than people think."

They walked together along a path where the bog had formed naturally—firm, flexible, responsive. Asa's steps no longer sharpened coherence behind him.

The world held itself.

"I won't stay everywhere," he said after a time.

"No," Saxifraga agreed. "Nor should you."

"But I'll return," he added.

"Yes."

They stopped where the living surface met open space, the basin spreading outward beyond sight.

"This isn't an ending," Asa said.

"No," Saxifraga replied. "It is a continuation that no longer requires us to begin it."

Chapter Eighteen

What Is Left in Trust

They spoke of the future without planning it.

Some worlds would open slowly. Others would never accept exchange in the same way. Life would move where it could, retreat where it must, and return again when readiness allowed.

Nothing would be forced.

The bees continued their cycles—Earth to basin, basin to Earth—never exhausting either place. The hives thrived. The bogs breathed.

And between them, something durable had formed.

Trust.

Saxifraga felt the ancient tension that had once defined her role ease into rest. She would remain—not as sole guardian, but as witness. Her presence would be felt only when needed.

Asa felt the opposite shift. His role would be motion, not settlement—returning, listening, adjusting, leaving again.

Neither path was greater.

They stood together at the threshold one last time.

"What if someone tries to control this?" Asa asked quietly.

Saxifraga did not hesitate. "They will fail."

"Because?"

"Because life no longer depends on permission."

Asa nodded. "Good."

Chapter Nineteen

She Sows

The title did not belong to a person.

Saxifraga understood that now.

Nor did it belong to the bees alone, or to the bogs, or even to the worlds that had waited so long to remember one another.

She was the act itself.

The choosing to place life gently into life.

The refusal to dominate what could instead be accompanied.

The patience to let growth decide its own shape.

Asa stood at the edge of the basin, watching the bees disappear into the fold and return again, each cycle leaving no scar behind.

"They'll keep doing this," he said. "Long after we're gone."

"Yes," Saxifraga replied. "That is the point."

She felt the network settle fully at last—not closed, not complete, but capable. The era of guardians had given way to the era of relationships.

What had been sown would continue to seed itself.

Epilogue

The Quiet Future

Far from the basins, far from Earth, a dormant gate shifted its attention.

Not opening.

Not calling.

Listening.

Somewhere, life would answer.

And when it did, there would be no announcement, no declaration of rescue or conquest.

Only the quiet movement of life toward life—

because it remembered how.

End of *She Sows*